ALPHABET ANATOMY

Learning your letters is easily done;
exploring their lives is a whole lot of fun!

Meet the Lower Case Letters

Nathan: My love follows you to the ends of the universe.

About this Book

Amusing rhymes and illustrations provide a simple visual and auditory method for letter mastery as children unlock the mystery of the letters' shapes.

By giving life to each letter based on its shape, the rhymes playfully teach the letter components with the creative construction of verses that depict how the letters spend their time…, when they're not busy doing their main job of making words.

Rhymes play an integral part in helping children develop critical thinking and memory skills, oral language, phonetic awareness, sound discrimination, and increased vocabulary, all of which are important building blocks of literacy.

The visual and auditory pictures created by the rhymes provide instruction on not only letter shape and sound but also the correct handwriting strokes required to form each letter, including forward, backward, downward, right, and left direction. For example:

- Letter a "acts like an acrobat" and practices her back somersault. A child can thus visualize the backward circular handwriting stroke and downward stroke that are required to form letter a, as if she were doing her back somersault.

- Letter r "likes to pretend he's a rabbit or hare." In doing so, he jumps down, then hops right, but stops in mid-air. A child can thus recall the required downward, upward, and forward handwriting strokes to properly form letter r.

Notice that the capital letters are also hidden in the illustration portions of each lower case letter page. As you re-read the book, help your child recall the capital letters and note the similarities or differences between the two.

For lower case letters that look similar to or the same as their corresponding capital letters, these rhymes relate back to the capital letter rhyme in order to make that connection. For example:

- "b bites big burgers just like his dad, but he's 1 belly fat 'cause he eats just a tad. b – belly" (Capital letter B is similar.)

- "s stands like a snake, the same as her mother. Right now she's in trouble for biting her brother. s - stands" (Capital letter S is the same.)

Recite the rhymes early on in play and while engaged in games and other fun activities. Children learn best through playful experiences, all of which serve as a springboard for literacy.

Once your child is ready for more focused instruction, use the rhymes as a tool to teach beginning reading and handwriting.

Introduction

The lower case letters are here in this book
Each one is so happy you stopped by to look
You'll see how they spend a lot of their time
To help you remember, they made up a rhyme.

I think you'll agree letters do need a break
From the millions of words they're required to make
So when they're not busy employing their sound
Here's how you will find them all hanging around.

Did you know letter g enjoys going fishing
To ace somersaults is what letter a's wishing
Letter t helps his dad build the tree house so tall
Walking through town, letter i brings his ball.

Letter s says she's sorry for biting her brother
Caring for cats, letter c helps her mother
Letter n, you will notice, is tying his shoe
Letter k and her sis have a pet kangaroo.

When you see letters gathered together in print
There's always a message and you'll have a hint
Reading the rhymes will give you some clues
For the sound and the shape every letter must use.

As you meet all these letters in lower case size
Look close on each page to find a surprise
The capital letters are visiting too
It's a big jolly family, this whole letter crew.

So excited to help, they just know you'll succeed
For reading and writing are splendid indeed
They can hardly stand waiting to make their debut
And begin on this wonderful journey with you!

a acts like an acrobat aiming to ace
her back somersault, with beauty and grace.

a - acrobat

b bites big burgers just like his dad,
but he's 1 belly fat 'cause he eats just a tad.

b - belly

c looks like her mom, and her right side is best,
for cute cuddly cats to come inside and rest.

c - cuddly

d dives down straight with dynamic flair.
He does it so fast that his pants fill with air.

d – down

e endeavors a trick every eve in her bed.
She jumps over the top and curls under instead.

e - endeavors

f fashions a flip going backwards, you see,
then fastens his belt and smiles with glee.

f - flip

g has gone fishing, curled up in a ball.
His hook's left in the lake grabbing guppies so small.

g - guppies

h hops down and jumps right, playing hopscotch 'til noon,
while happily humming a humorous tune.

h - hopscotch

i walks straight as his ball idles up in the air.
No one can imagine just how it stays there.

i – imagine

j jokes as his hook hangs down left in the sea,
and a star overhead appears magically.

j - jokes

k flies a kite too, not as high as her sis,
and her pet kangaroo may blow her a kiss.

k - kangaroo

I has lovely posture, stands straight as can be.
He likes to laugh loudly but sometimes looks lonely.

I - lonely

m makes 2 jumps forward ahead of the crowd.
She maintains good manners but talks very loud.

m - manners

n never stops needing to tie his right shoe.
So he's always bent over, and proud of it too.

n - never

o operates circular just like her dad.
To overcome obstacles makes them both glad.

o - operates

p plunges down in the pool at the park.
Then his belly puffs out 'cause he swallowed a shark.

p - pool

q does a quick back roll, then dives in the lake.
He does not get queasy and stays wide awake.

q - quick

r likes to pretend he's a rabbit or hare.
He jumps down, then hops right, but stops in mid-air.

r - rabbit

s stands like a snake, the same as her mother.
Right now she's in trouble for biting her brother.

s - stands

t stands tall like his dad, but won't use his head.
He tends to haul timber on his shoulders instead.

t - tall

u looks like his uncle but stays on the land.
And he usually uses his right leg to stand.

u - uncle

v veers down the valley, just like her big sis.
And she ventures to say, "there's just no place like this."

v - veers

w looks the same as her mother.
In her wagon, she gives wild rides to her brother.

w - wild

x likes x-ing stuff out, just like his brother.
They're best friends and never get cross at each other.

x - x-ing

y yawns with both arms raised high to stay cool.
She leaves her right leg hanging left in the pool.

y - yawns

z zips the zig-zag the same as his dad.
He rips his pants too, and his mom won't be glad.

z – zips

Hooray!

You met lower case letters a through z
And learned about their lives in...

ALPHABET ANATOMY!

The letters look forward to seeing you again!

Nurture Early Literacy

Each day is filled with countless opportunities to enrich your child's early literacy foundation simply by engaging in meaningful conversations and facilitating playful learning experiences.

Alphabet Anatomy's rhymes and illustrations also serve as a premise for further discussion, storytelling, and creative fun:

- Ask your child questions about the letters and their activities.
- Make connections between the letters' activities and your child's own experiences.
- Identify and discuss the letters in your child's name.
- Name all the colors and objects on each page.
- Think of more rhyming words for each letter's verse.
- Make up additional stories about the letters.
- Draw story pictures about the letters and their activities.
- Repeat each letter's sound and key word; use the key word in a sentence.
- Trace each letter as the rhyme is read and write it in the air.
- Find the capital letter on each page and write that in the air too.

Encourage and grow a literacy rich environment:

- Letters are all around us! Point them out at home, while driving and shopping, and everywhere you see them.
- Play games that build letter and sound knowledge. For instance, how many words can you think of that begin with the letter c?
- Read lots of books and other rhymes together.
- Introduce new vocabulary words and explain their meanings.
- Encourage writing attempts, beginning with your child's name, and incorporate it into activities and routines.
- Model writing - for example, lists and messages.
- Sing songs and make up your own.
- Create a treasure hunt for letters or other objects.
- Go for walks; draw pictures or write about all that you see.
- Make simple crafts with household items such as empty food boxes, cartons, paper towel rolls, styrofoam cups, ribbon/string/yarn, and paper plates.
- Create your own alphabet book and other themed books with magazine pictures, or draw your own.
- Keep a craft box stocked with scissors, glue sticks, crayons, markers, assorted paper, cards, felt pieces, buttons, and other decorative items to inspire creative art and develop fine-motor skills.

Provide assorted methods and materials for writing the letters:

- Flour on the kitchen counter
- Shaving cream in the bathtub
- Salt in a cake pan or baking dish
- Sand in a basin or sandbox
- Finger motions in the air
- Finger-painting on paper
- Molding letters with play-dough
- Highlighted letters for tracing

Made in the USA
Lexington, KY
25 February 2015